SEQUIN and Stitch

Laura Dockrill

Illustrated by
Sara Ogilvie

Barrington Stoke

First published in 2020 in Great Britain by
Barrington Stoke Ltd
18 Walker Street, Edinburgh, EH3 7LP

www.barringtonstoke.co.uk

Text © 2020 Laura Dockrill
Illustrations © 2020 Sara Ogilvie

A CIP catalogue record for this book is available
from the British Library upon request

ISBN: 978-1-78112-931-9

Printed in China by Leo

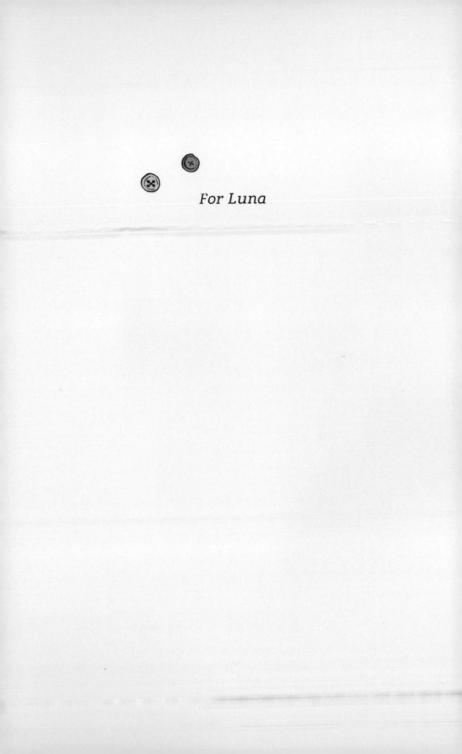

For Luna

Chapter 1

I live in Primrose Mansions.

It doesn't look like how a *real* mansion is meant to look. It's tall and cold and grey and split into lots of small flats.

If you look at our building from far away, it looks like a remote control for a giant's TV – a big rectangle standing up on one end, covered in teensy window buttons.

And we live all the way up on the twelfth floor.

Me. Mum. And my baby brother, Stitch.

Up here I can pretend I'm the princess of the city, sitting on my throne. Looking down on the world from my high tower.

We are safe up here. Hidden in our fortress. Mum and me and baby Stitch.

And our home *is* a special palace.

It is.

I'll tell you why.

Chapter 2

My mum is probably one of the most important people on the planet. But it's difficult because she doesn't even know it. You see, my mum is a "maker" and that means she "makes" stuff with her hands. She makes clothes. And not just any clothes. She makes magnificent ball gowns and glorious frocks, fancy three-piece suits and decorated quilted coats.

You know those amazing outfits that famous people wear on the red carpet at film premieres and award parties? Guess who makes them?

My mum!

Have you seen the dresses the women in perfume adverts in magazines wear as they spread out across sofas? Guess who makes them?

Yep, my mum!

She works so hard, night after night, crouched over her desk under the peachy lamp in our living room. She sips tea after tea, sews stitch after stitch, bead after bead, embroidering and braiding, lacing and hemming and bordering. She works until her fingers bleed and her back aches and she is so tired she says she can "see stars".

The beads and sequins on the clothes make me feel as if I'm surrounded by a princess's precious jewellery. So, to me, our flat is a palace. And it's perfect.

Well, all apart from our annoying downstairs neighbour, grumpy Moany Bony Mr Tony (I'm not allowed to call him that to his face). He smokes one billion and five cigarettes a day and makes our palace stink with the stench of them. He used to smoke indoors and that was bad because the smell seeped in through the ceiling. So then we asked him to smoke on the balcony and it got even worse as we can hardly ever open the windows now. But we're too scared to tell him because he's so miserable. Moany Bony Mr Tony absolutely hates life (and us) and always bangs on our floor with a broomstick when we have the TV too loud or do too much dancing or jumping.

He shouts, "WILL YOU KEEP THAT BLEEDIN' RACKET DOWN?!"

And we shout back, "SORRY, TONY!"

Even though he should really be the one saying sorry to us for making our home smell like an old boot.

I said to Mum that Moany Bony Mr Tony should give up smoking because it's really bad for him. But Mum said that sometimes people need something bad to make them feel good.

And I said, "What? Like me and sweets?"

And she said, "Exactly – like you and sweets."

"I think Moany Bony Mr Tony fancies Mum,"
I whisper to Stitch. But Stitch is just a baby, so
he says nothing back.

Not that it matters. Mum would never ever
ever fancy Moany Bony Mr Tony's old wrinkled
face and his bloodshot eyes. Not to mention
his smelly old beard that is kind of white but
stained brown like it's been dipped in a cup of
tea.

Chapter 3

The dresses that Mum makes are my favourite.

The more sparkly and magical and fairy-tale-like the better.

The colours of the fabrics that she uses are so amazing that I completely forget I'm looking at a piece of clothing. Instead the folds of emerald and jade velvet and silk transport me to a rich tropical rainforest.

When I see the dresses being made from scratch, it's like watching a jungle grow from just a tiny seed before my very eyes. I know it sounds silly, as they are just dresses, but it's true. Layers and layers come together to make something so real and magnificent. It's easy to get attached to the clothes, as if they have personalities.

And then all of a sudden the outfits are ready, after they've lived in our flat for *all* this time.

They must leave us and Primrose Mansions.

And it's like they never existed at all.

It's a bit like losing a friend really.

And I can't think of many things sadder than that.

I'm sure there are sadder things.

I just can't think of them right this second.

I often say to Mum, "I love this one *so* much. Can't we keep it? *Please?*" and she just laughs and says how expensive the dresses are. We would never be able to afford *one* of those dresses, not even if we saved up for our whole entire lives.

When Mum has finished an outfit, it's my job to find as many photographs of the person wearing the dress or suit as I can. I look in magazines and newspapers and cut them out and pin them on the wall.

Our wall is covered with pictures showing Mum's years of work. It's like an archive – a record of everything she's made. It's an art gallery containing all that is amazing about my mum's clever brain.

I always search for her name in the magazines ... but I never see it, ever.

Only the designer's name appears.

That's who Mum works for.

I don't know how the designer can live
with that. It's a bit like taking somebody

else's drawing and writing your name on it, pretending it was drawn by you.

And so the world will never know that it isn't the designers that make the beautiful clothes.

It's actually my mum.

But *I* know.

And so does Stitch.

And now I guess you all know too.

And that is why my mum is *my* inspiration.

Chapter 4

I am Sequin.

And I am nine.

And everything I've just told you was a speech I gave at school.

I read it out in front of *everyone* in my class.

Which is brave for me because I don't like talking out loud in front of everybody, especially not at school.

But I did it because at school we are learning about *inspiration*.

Inspiration is a pretty difficult word to explain but it's a good word to know. When you are inspired by something or someone, it means that you are so impressed by their amazingness that it makes *you* want to do something amazing too.

Our teacher Mr Moore asked us to think about what *inspires* us. And then we were asked to give a presentation on it.

Alice said her inspiration was her grandma. She is now an old lady but when she was young she was a nurse. Zaynab chose a YouTuber. Teegan said her inspiration was Mr Moore (because she is an annoying teacher's pet). David Fisher chose food. Sophia chose the pyramids in Egypt. And Amir chose his great-great-great-uncle who was a scientist.

Mum blushed like a grape and shook her head when I first said I was going to do my inspiration presentation on *her*.

But then she realised that I was serious and helped me look in her wonderful scrap box. This is a big plastic box full to the brim of odd bits and offcuts of material: silk, cotton, lace, velvet, Lycra, crepe. I wanted to make a big collage of Mum's fabrics to show everybody at school. We rummaged in the box like we were digging for treasure, to find tabs and rags and squares of fabric. We stuck them on a big roll of display paper that was *so* big I needed Mr Moore to help me hold it up.

While we were sticking the fabric down, all I could think about was how much my class would not believe their eyes or ears when I told them how clever and creative my mum was.

How we had so much fabric at home!

How my mum made dresses for people in magazines and famous people on red carpets too.

They would not believe me at all.

Chapter 5

After my presentation, Teegan from school calls me a liar in front of everyone.

She says in this horrible little voice, "I asked *my* mum about *you*, Sequin, *and* your *weird* mum. She said that if your mum *really* made all of those dresses for all them famous people, then you lot would be millionaires living in a *real* mansion, not some rubbish estate like Primrose Mansions."

I shake my head and say, "That's not true, Teegan."

Now Fatima joins in. "Do you have *any* idea how much those dresses cost, Sequin? Like thousands and thousands and millions of pounds. Your family would be rich if you were telling the truth."

"I am telling the truth," I reply, defending myself, my mum, Stitch and all of the dresses too. Wet gluey tears build in my eyes and my knees feel weak and wobbly.

"Well, anyway, it's not good to be a show-off." Fatima talks down to me like a teacher.

"Yeah, nobody likes a show-off," Olivia pipes up. "Just saying."

Oh, shut up, Olivia, I think.

"I wasn't showing off!" I argue. "The presentation was for school!"

"*It was for school,*" Teegan mimics me.

Everyone knows you only mimic someone when you can't think of anything else to say.

Olivia sniggers to impress Teegan.

"Maybe Teegan's right, Sequin," Fatima says, and shrugs. "Maybe you *are* a liar."

"NO, I AM NOT!"

"Yes, you are!" Teegan snarls. "Or then why are you so poor?"

I say nothing and look down at my beaten-up shoes. I should have said, *Well, why are you so horrible?* But I think of that too late.

Teegan's face is going purple – the same purple as the heart-shaped beaded bodice my mum made the actress Swana Lee for the premiere of *Love Loss*. Teegan spits, "I reckon you just *pretend* your weird mum does all of that sewing stuff because your stupid name is Sequin and you're just embarrassed. Or maybe your mum's just mad?"

This stings.

I feel like I've been slapped right round the face, yet nobody has even touched me. My face tingles with blood but it feels like electricity and my eyes water. The words hurt. People have called my mum "mad" before, but that doesn't make it hurt any less. They are only stupid rumours. Mum's not mad. She's just shy. That's all.

"My mum isn't mad," I tell them. "And she's not weird."

"Then how come she *never* leaves the house?" Teegan demands.

OUCH.

I don't know the answer to that.

She just doesn't like to leave the flat. What's the problem with that?

I suppose sometimes it is weird.

I'm never allowed any friends over. Everything has to be ordered online and delivered. Mum never comes to meet me at the school gates. She's never come to the Christmas play.

I say nothing.

"Yeah. Thought so. *Weird*." Teegan smirks and walks away.

Nobody sticks up for me.

Everybody is too scared to stand up to scary Teegan.

Some people in my class feel sorry for me, I can tell. But I don't like it when people feel sorry for me. It just makes me feel worse.

When I really think about it, our flat is a palace to me ... but for Mum it's a prison, with the windows sealed shut. It's like she's chained to the walls. The chains are invisible yet they're stronger than any metal and I can't think of how to break her free from their grasp.

Chapter 6

Stitch is happy I am home from school. I scoop him up and sit him up on my lap. I squeeze his plump cheeks and blow noises on his round tummy and kiss him to absolute death. He always knows how to make me feel better because I can say things to him I can't say to anybody at school. He understands even though he's just a tiny baby.

Mum has got some news.

"Sequin," she says, "sit down. I have some really exciting news to tell you."

I hold my breath, then gasp, "What is it?"

"We've got a new job."

"OK ..."

I can tell this is going to be good ...

"It's a big one," Mum says.

I get excited. This is probably the *best* bit about Mum's job. Finding out what she is going to make next!

A feathered corset for an actress's fancy dinner party? A frock for a jewellery advert? A shimmering fairy-tale ball gown? A ballerina's skirt?

"Sequin ... I have been asked to make the PRINCESS'S WEDDING DRESS ... for the royal wedding!"

WHAT?

"MUM!" I jump up and down.

I lift Stitch up and swirl him around in the air; he gargles with delight.

"WOW! WOW! WOW!" I say, and hug Mum tight. "This is the dream job for you! Ahhhhh! What are the ideas? What colours? What shape? I can't wait to see the drawings. When do you start?"

"Calm down!" Mum giggles. "I will show you *everything*, but it's a big job. It's going to take a lot of work and a lot of time. I am going to be very busy, so I wanted to make sure you'd be OK with that."

"Mum, yes! Of course I'm OK with that. I can help."

"Ah, I know you will. Thank you, Quinny."

"I will," I say. "I'll help with threading the needle and all the delicate bits and picking up any tiny pins—"

"OK, my lovely." Mum smiles. "That will really help."

"And I'll take care of Stitch too, so you don't have to worry about him." I run over to Mum's wall and start looking at ideas. "Oh, Mum, this is so GREAT! I can't WAIT to tell everybody at school that you're making the real-life royal wedding dress for the actual princess!"

"Ah, that's another thing," Mum says. "We aren't allowed to tell anybody about this one."

"Ohhh. Why not?"

"It's very private and special, Sequin. I know we're excited but it's traditional for a wedding dress to be kept a secret."

"But, Mum ... it's the *princess*," I say. "I have to tell someone!"

YEAH, LIKE ANNOYING TEEGAN!

"This is the royal wedding dress, Sequin. People will try to get a sneaky peek of it however they can. If even one photograph of the dress gets out, the whole thing will be ruined. It's very important that the designers trust us, that it remains a secret. So we have to be patient, OK?"

"OK." I slump down at the table.

"Promise?" Mum asks.

"Promise." I begin to fiddle with the stem of an apple from the fruit bowl.

"Will your name be mentioned?" I ask. I sort of know this question will annoy her but it would give me proof that Mum does really make all the famous people's clothes. Then everybody would know that I'm not a liar. They'd know that my mum is actually important.

Mum raises her eyebrows and gives me a knowing look.

"Sequin, not this again," Mum says. "You know it doesn't work like that. It's the designer's name they want in the magazines, not mine."

"Yeah, but you're the one that does all the work! *Mum!* Come on, it's the royal wedding dress! You deserve to be mentioned. At least *think* about asking them."

"OK, I'll think about it."

"Promise?" I ask.

"Promise."

"Well, that's a promise each then." I nod, then bite into one of the apples. I spit out the mouthful fast. Mum frowns at me.

"*What?* It was mushy and brown tasting!" I say.

Mum points to the bin and I plod over and do as I'm told.

"How did your inspiration presentation go at school?" Mum asks.

I hesitate. I want to tell Mum about Teegan but I don't want to make her feel bad and spoil her good news. "I think *everybody* was inspired by you, Mum," I say. "You're so amazing, they almost couldn't believe it."

She laughs. "I don't know about that." She strokes my hair and adds, "You're very sweet to do the talk about me, Quinny. It means a lot to me. I love you."

"I love you too, Mum." I can't help but yelp out another squeal of excitement.

"MUM! YOU'RE MAKING THE ROYAL PRINCESS'S WEDDING DRESS!"

We jump up and down all over again.

And then we hear the broomstick beating on the floor. Moany Bony Mr Tony from downstairs shouts, "WILL YOU KEEP THAT BLEEDIN' RACKET DOWN?!"

"Sorry, Tony!" we sing, and then we giggle and poke our tongues out at the floor.

*

When I'm rocking Stitch to sleep later on, I imagine the princess coming to collect me from school with Mum. She gives the door a high kick in her beautiful wedding dress and shows them all that everything I've said about Mum is true.

That would shut up Teegan and her annoying mum.

Then they'd be sorry.

Chapter 7

Over the next few weeks, our doorbell rings constantly with deliveries of materials and tools for Mum. Opening each box is like the best surprise ever – over and over again.

Mum is so busy, she barely has a chance to look up.

She's already made the wedding veil. It is like a *huge* fishing net that you might catch a *gigantic* blue whale inside. It has millions of individually stitched petal shapes scattered all over it – pink, coral, yellow and lavender. They are detailed and delicate, like blossom. Mum and I shake the veil out and it spreads across our whole living room, floating in the air like a rainbow.

We hang it up with clothes pegs on a washing line across the flat. Stitch lies beneath it, his legs kicking and his button eyes staring up at the canopy above.

We can no longer see the TV but we don't care – the veil is way more interesting. We have to hop across the living room to make sure that we don't step on anything precious. It's like we are leaping across shark-infested waters. We pass Stitch across the room like he's a parcel and watch him at all times so he doesn't put any beads or pins into his mouth.

Mum says that when I'm older I will be able to do lots more sewing and stuff if I want to. But the princess's dress is just so precious and the materials are so expensive that Mum can't afford to make any mistakes or let me help.

But she *does* let me thread the needle for her in preparation for the fine needlework. It's easier for me because my hands are so small. The eye of the sharp needle winks at me. I take great care, my eyes squinted, tongue out, a frown on my face even though I'm not cross. I'm just trying to do a good job for my mum – and for the princess too, of course. The needle slides down the golden thread like a pendant on a necklace. Like it was always meant to be there. And I feel so proud because *I* threaded the needle for a dress that is going to be worn by an actual princess.

I watch Mum work while Stitch sleeps on the sofa behind us. His puffy mouth is like a heart-shaped bruise in a kiss, the soft warm glow of Mum's working lamp lighting up his angel cheeks. I fight off sleep – I'm falling in and out of a dream. Eventually Mum says, "It really is time for bed now, Quinny."

I want to resist but I know she's already let me stay up way past my bedtime to help with the dress. So I kiss her goodnight, knowing she'll be up for hours. The radio will babble quietly in the background; tea and biscuits will keep her company.

I fall asleep with Stitch gently snoring next to me, his baby chest rising and falling. I'm excited for the next morning, when Mum will have done *even* more work to the dress.

And I can't *wait* to see it.

It's like my birthday every morning.

Chapter 8

Mum has to have many meetings with the designer about the dress.

It *is* the royal wedding dress after all.

Mum doesn't like the designers and stylists coming over to our flat.

Mum doesn't like *anybody* coming over.

Sometimes she's scared of people a bit.

But secretly I like it when people come over. If it was up to me, we'd have guests here all the time. We could make them tea and pasta pesto.

Maybe I can show the designer my glitter wand and my slime? I could show them how good I am at threading needles.

We put the rough sample of the princess's dress on a mannequin, which is like a dolly the size of an adult, without a head. It's not scary. It's just so the designers can see what the dress will look like on a person.

We have to keep the windows shut tight the whole entire time so that none of Moany Bony Mr Tony's smoke gets in. It's *so* stuffy.

Stitch and I watch from the crack in the door of my bedroom.

The designers talk in annoying posh voices and say stuff that doesn't even make sense. They don't drink our tea from our cups. They all have takeaway coffee cups. They *always* make changes to Mum's work, *even* when it's already perfect.

"Don't worry," I whisper to Stitch. "They *always* do that. It's just so they feel important."

I don't think the designers would be interested in my glitter wand. Or the slime. Or watching me thread the needle.

When they leave, Mum clears away their cardboard coffee cups and starts to make dinner. Sausages and mash with gravy and peas.

"Did you ask them about having your name in the magazines this time?" I ask Mum.

But I know she didn't.

Mum begins to cry.

"Oh no, don't cry," I say. "Mum, what's the matter? Why are you crying?"

"Sorry, I'm not crying." (She definitely is.) "I just get so embarrassed when they come round ..."

"Embarrassed? About what?" I ask.

"You know ... about *me* ... about *the flat*."

"Why? We have the greatest flat ever in the whole wide world! I know it's ugly on the outside but it's beautiful on the inside and that's what counts! And you, Mum? You're just the best."

"Oh, Sequin, you're so lovely."

"No, you are!" I tell Mum. "Our flat is! Look how lovely it is here, Mum. Look how lovely you've made it. Look at all your amazing wonderful drawings on the wall. Look at all the magazine pictures of your clothes, your fabrics and materials. Look how clever you are. I love it here. It's our home. It's warm and cosy and creative and happy and safe! It's YOU. In a flat!"

"Oh, thank you, Quinny. I know." Mum cuddles me and kisses me on the forehead.

"You're right. It is our home. I love it too. It's just ... most of the professionals have fancy studios and I ... Oh, I'm being silly ... Sometimes I think that if I had a fancy studio I'd be taken a bit more seriously. That the designers would ... I don't know ... *prefer* it if I was *different*."

"No, Mum, they don't care *where* you work. It's *you* they want. Not a studio."

I wipe her tears away.

"And *if* they want you to have a fancy posh studio," I add, "then they should pay you more money so you can have one!"

Mum tuts. "Sequin, not this again."

"It's true. The girls at school told me how much the dresses you make cost. Where does all that money go, Mum? Why don't you get any of it?"

"I'm too *low* down," Mum says.

"How are you low down? You're the highest, Mum – you can't get higher than up here in our flat!"

We laugh, looking out at the city from our view. It gives me the guts to ask Mum, "Maybe it would be good to have people over sometimes?"

"Who?" Mum asks. She looks shocked that I even suggested it.

"I don't know ... friends? Then maybe it wouldn't feel so scary?"

"I don't think so, Sequin. What friends anyway? I haven't got any!" Mum smiles but I know she's sad.

"OK, well, what about us going out somewhere?" I suggest. "Wouldn't it be nice to go out for once? The three of us? Like a ... normal family?"

"That's the problem, Sequin," Mum says. "I don't think we're very normal."

I feel sick. It's like Mum herself is sewn into the walls of the flat and the thread just seems to get tighter and thicker. She's like a spider caught in her own sticky web. I want to run away. I want to scream I HATE YOU and slam the door on her.

But I don't.

I crawl into bed with Stitch and cry into his soft face.

Chapter 9

Saturdays are normally the best days ever, but this one is not much fun.

In just one week, the wedding dress is being collected for the princess to try it on. The designers and stylist are coming here on Monday for the final reveal.

And Mum is stressed.

It's raining so much that I can't even take Stitch outside in his pushchair, so we feel all trapped, like we are in a boiling saucepan. We aren't allowed the TV on because Mum needs to concentrate. And we can't eat any hot food because Mum doesn't want any of the cooking smells leaking into the fabric.

"Mum, I'm bored," I say.

"Sequin, I'm under a lot of pressure here. It's the final push now."

"But, Mum, can't I just help you one tiny bit?"

"Sequin, I've told you," Mum says. "NO!"

I'm annoyed.

It's *my* home too.

And I've taken care of Stitch all by myself.

How come all the designers earn loads of money and get to have their own swimming pools and we don't? For a second I want to rip up that stupid princess dress, but I know that would ruin Mum's whole entire life, so I don't.

I scream really fast into a blanket and stomp back into the living room. Mum has pins in her mouth and her eyebrows are all knitted together. I eat *more* cream cheese sandwiches – the most *boring silent unstinkiest* food *ever* – and then I dress Stitch up in different outfits from Mum's scrap box. I pin and stitch him like he's my model and I'm a designer at the catwalk.

"FABULOUS, GORGEOUS, DARLING!!" I say.

Stitch just sits there smiling and I'm careful not to prick his soft velvet skin with any of the needles.

Before bath time, Mum says I'm allowed a FULL HOUR of craziness because I've been "so good" all day and "very patient". But we mustn't be in the living room where the dress is, because it's very delicate and fragile. The tiniest of vibrations could shake the beading and make the lace tremble and tear.

I take full advantage of this opportunity and dance around the kitchen banging on the pots and pans. I totally ignore Moany Bony Mr Tony's annoying stupid broomstick banging, because we've been nothing but silent all day long.

Afterwards, I'm in the bubble bath pretending to be a mermaid and Mum knocks on the door with the greatest treat ever.

A *massive* ham and pineapple takeaway pizza to eat *in the bath*!

I clap my hands like a seal.

"Sorry for snapping at you," Mum says.

"You're forgiven," I say, and bite into my cheesy pizza. "It's all worth it."

"I hope so."

"Are you going to ask them on Monday?" I say. "To mention you?"

"Yes," says Mum.

"Do you promise?"

"Yes, I promise."

Chapter 10

Stitch and I wake up on Sunday morning and see Mum sitting at the end of my bed. She's beaming proudly as the sun filters through the curtains.

"OK, it's ready ..." Mum whispers excitedly. I can tell she's hardly slept.

Mum leads me into the living room with her overworked hands covering my eyes. "No peeking ..."

My heart is beating.

"Ready ... steady ... go ..." Mum says.

And she removes her hands for me to see the finished royal wedding dress on the mannequin.

The dress is like a dazzling chandelier, shimmering and glinting and twinkling. It's a mirror ball of diamonds, throwing confetti reflections onto the walls of our cramped flat, jewel sparkles hanging from the ceiling like tears.

Or it's a white silent blanket of snow, with glittering snowflakes of ivory lace. It's like lashings of thick frosty icing on a Christmas cake, but light like whipped ice cream. It's a mosaic of glass beads, swan-like silk, of pearl sequins.

It is *perfect*.

"You've done it, Mum!" I say. "You've done it!"

Mum admires her work and smiles, which she doesn't often do. "All I have to do now," she says, "is find the courage to convince Moany Bony Mr Tony not to smoke for the rest of the day. Otherwise the princess is going to walk down the aisle smelling like an ashtray."

"Don't worry about that, Mum. I'll ask him."

*

I don't need to use the lift for one floor. I don't really like the lift anyway. Stitch does – he likes the lights and the buttons. But that's because he's such a tiny baby and anything impresses him.

I clatter down the stone stairs of Primrose Mansions where it's all cold and stinky and echoey. My trainers smack on the floor. I have to be extra careful with Stitch under my arm, because if he fell his head would crack. The steps are made of concrete but if you look closely there are specks of glitter hidden in the grey. The banisters have been painted over and over so many times that the paint has cracked off. In places you can see layers and layers of different colours under the plain black paint.

I can already smell the stink of Moany Bony Mr Tony's smoky cigarette flat leaking into the halls.

His doormat is old and hairy and scruffy. Written on it in big black letters are the words, "GO AWAY!"

I take a deep breath and *rat-a-tat-tat* on Moany Bony Mr Tony's door, then I grip Stitch tight and wait.

"Ello? Who are ya?" a gravelly voice thunders through the door.

"It's Sequin and Stitch, from upstairs?" I say.

I hear nothing. And then a clank and clang of different locks and bolts being undone.

The whiff of stale smoke and ash rolls out from Moany Bony Mr Tony's front door. The darkness of his scraggy flat is like a gloomy ghostly fog hanging over a forest. We wait for his yellowy-browny dirty skinny fingers to creep around the front door.

"WOT?" Moany Bony Mr Tony grunts. "Don't you know I hate kids?"

He sniffs me like I'm a piece of rotten fish and glares at me with his scary veiny eyes. He is wearing old brown trousers covered in oily marks and a stained yellow shirt.

"Well, what does she want this time?" he demands, talking about my mum.

And I have to just smile. "Sorry, Tony, but Mum's got some important fabric upstairs that—" I say it in my most polite voice, not that it matters much with Moany Bony Mr Tony.

"You don't want it smellin' like fags. Make your bleedin' mind up! I get it."

And he slams the door in my face.

"Thanks, Moany Bony Mr Tony."

"What'd you call me?" he shouts from inside.

"Errrr ... nothing," I say, and I skip off back upstairs.

Chapter 11

When I get back from school on Monday, the designers are here again – with their posh voices and takeaway coffee cups.

Stitch and I listen from the kitchen, peeking our heads around the door. I lick peanut butter off the back of a spoon.

This time they don't say annoying stuff. They don't make annoying laughs. Or sounds.

They are totally silent.

At first I think it's because they are angry with Mum.

But they are stunned.

The head designer says, "I have never
seen anything so spectacular in my whole
life. I knew you were good, but I had no idea
a human was capable of such work."

Mum blushes.

"I would never normally say this, but ..."
the royal stylist adds. "Instead of us taking the
dress to the palace, I wonder ... if we could bring
the princess here to meet you – to try the dress
on with you. Would you be happy with that?"

"The princess? Coming *here* to *our* flat?"
Mum asks, shocked. She is stuttering and
backtracking and already shaking her head.
I see her grip the back of the chair to steady
herself. Her other hand is on her chest like she
is trying to keep her breath in. I peek my head
out further and Mum catches my eyes with
hers.

"Would that be OK?" the royal stylist asks again.

Mum chokes. I nod at her, telling her to say *yes, yes, say yes*. "But ... my flat ..." Mum says. "It's ... a bit ... you know?"

"Oh, *please* ... the princess *adores* shabby chic," the royal stylist tells her.

Shabby chic? Our flat's a palace! I want to shout.

"OK, if you're sure, in that case ... I suppose." Mum nods.

WOW.

The designer and stylist hug my mum and take photographs of the dress with them all standing next to it. Then they shake her hand and say she'll hear from them *very* soon to talk about the *future*.

"This is going to change my whole career – you're my secret weapon!" the designer says to Mum. "I'm so pleased we found you. Thanks again. See you soon."

GO ON, MUM! I will her to speak. *This is when you ask to be named in the magazines. This is when you remind them that the princess's dress is YOUR work ... Mum?*

But Mum doesn't. She says goodbye and then tidies up their takeaway coffee cups.

Great.

Now I'll never be able to prove to anybody how wonderful Mum is.

Now I'll always be a liar. A liar with a weirdo for a mum.

Chapter 12

Mum tucks me in bed, we rub noses and she switches the light off. We are plunged into darkness for a tiny second before she flicks on my star nightlight and its familiar blue ray shines out.

Mum flops onto my bed and asks, "Why don't you try sleeping on your own tonight, Quinny?"

"I like it when Stitch sleeps with me," I say.

"But you're almost ten."

"So ... what does that mean?"

"Well, you'll be at big school in a year," Mum says. "And … it's nice to have your own space?"

"Where will Stitch sleep?" I ask.

Mum gives a deep sigh.

"Mum, can I bring a friend home soon?"

"Shall we talk about it once everything has calmed down a bit?"

"But what about *this* week?" I say.

"Quinny, you know nobody can see the princess's dress before the wedding."

"Just *one* friend? It will be so quick."

"I'm afraid not, Sequin," Mum says. "I signed a contract to keep it secret, and you know I can't go against that."

"But my friend won't say anything."

"I'm sure they won't, but I have to be so careful. You've been so patient up until now, Sequin. Just a little while longer and then we can tell the whole world."

"But we can't," I say. "Because nobody will know you even made it. You promised you would ask to be named and you didn't. You broke *your* promise." My voice is getting louder.

"Why are you so angry, Sequin?" Mum asks.

"Why don't you ever stand up for yourself? Why don't you care that nobody knows your name? Why do you just stay inside and not see anybody and why do you work so hard for other people? It's like you don't exist."

Mum folds my hair behind my ear and tucks Stitch in closer to me.

"Listen, you ..." Mum says. "We've got an actual real-life princess coming to *our* home. How many of your friends can say that?" She goes out of the room and I cling to Stitch. Eventually I drift off to sleep.

Chapter 13

I dream of a princess that night. She had everything a princess could possibly want – even a bedroom in the highest room in her grand castle. She thought her princess life couldn't get any more princess-ish, but then she met her prince charming. They fell in love. And they were soon to be wed.

The king and queen were very excited. They got the world's best wedding planners in to arrange the event. They had the best twinkling wedding rings made, the prince had his suit tailored, the bridesmaids had their dresses fitted and the flowers were all sorted. But there was *one thing* they could not find.

The perfect wedding dress.

Designers were flown in from all over the world to measure the princess and show her their grand visions for her dress. But they were just never quite right.

Each dress was too dark, too bright, too itchy, too silky, too swishy, too posh, too relaxed, too short, too long, too loose, too tight, too busy, too simple, too crazy or too boring.

The princess was tempted to get married in her cosy ice-cream onesie – at least it was comfortable.

One day the princess was in town getting her nails manicured and feeling rather deflated as she still didn't have a dress to get married in. Then she spotted the strangest thing she'd ever seen.

A flash of colour in the shape of a ladder.

Rung after rung made of every fabric hanging from the block of flats opposite.

The material was twisted and knotted – rags and scraps were braided and plaited. It was like a long friendship bracelet, dangling out of the sky …

"Sorry," the princess said to the nail technician as she got up. "I just need to …"

"Where are you going, Princess?" the technician asked. "Your nails … they're still wet! I haven't finished – they'll smudge."

The princess walked out of the nail bar as if locked in some strange trance. She began to climb the ladder of beautiful fabric, like she was hypnotised.

Floor one, two, three …

"PRINCESS!" shouted her security guards. "GET DOWN FROM THERE! IT'S VERY DANGEROUS!"

But the princess ignored them and kept climbing up the ladder.

The howling sound of sirens rang out.

But the princess kept climbing.

Floor four, five, six …

The princess was getting high now and the wind blew in her hair. A crowd began to watch.

"What *is* she doing?" someone asked.

"Has the princess lost her mind?" another said.

"Who even lives all the way up there?"

"What could the princess possibly want from a big ugly grey building like that?"

The people below the princess looked tiny to her, like lost pinheads on the carpet.

Floor seven, eight, nine ...

News reporters began to gather.

An emergency helicopter chugged overhead and a tinny voice from a megaphone shouted, "PRINCESS, PLEASE COME DOWN FROM THE LADDER. YOU ARE PUTTING YOUR LIFE IN DANGER. WE ARE COMING TO GET YOU."

But the princess kept climbing all the way up the block of flats. At the twelfth floor, she politely knocked on the window and clambered in.

Inside, all was silent. Apart from the princess's beating heart.

WOW.

Never in her life had the princess seen beauty like it. Costume after costume, dress after dress, suit after suit. They were all so majestic and spectacular that tears came to her eyes.

And there, sitting on the sofa, happily stitching away, was *Mum*.

It was as if she'd been waiting for the princess to pay her a visit.

The princess gazed at the dresses, totally mesmerised.

"May I?" she asked as her fingers tingled.

"Please do," said Mum.

By now a big crowd had gathered on the road beneath the block of flats. This included the prince, who was sweating – it was a pretty stressful situation for him. His future in-laws, the king and queen, were clinging to one another in fear. Everybody was very worried. Where had the princess gone? Had she been kidnapped?

And who owned this strange ladder in the sky?

Eventually, the princess emerged from the window wearing the most wondrous wedding gown anybody had ever seen! It was so stunning it nearly blinded people with its beauty.

It was a work of ART.

The princess started to climb back down the ladder, calling out, "I have met my seamstress, the most talented dressmaker in the whole world ... Sequin and Stitch's mum!"

Our mum appeared at the window. And the crowd went wild. The king and queen cried with joy and clapped their hands. And the prince wept and blew kisses up to his beautiful future wife at the window.

"Your flat is a palace! You look so beautiful, Princess!" the prince said.

And everybody was saying *"Thank you!"* to Mum.

And everybody was taking photos of Mum.

And everybody knew Mum's name.

And Teegan from school was there.

And Fatima.

And Olivia.

And they said, "Sorry we didn't believe you, Sequin."

And I said, "It's OK. Not everybody believes in magic until they *actually* see it."

And then I felt warmth all around me—

"SEQUIN! SEQUIN! WAKE UP … WAKE UP!
SEQUIN! SEQUIN! IT'S OUR BLOCK … SEQUIN,
IT'S ON FIRE!"

Chapter 14

There's panic in Mum's voice. Horrible panic. She rips me out of bed. I feel her pulsing heartbeat on my hand, drumming out of her chest.

"We've got to get out," Mum cries. "I've got you. It's going to be OK, Sequin, but it'll be a tiny bit scary before that, OK?"

I nod.

"Now, you need to stay with me the entire time and do everything I tell you to do," Mum says. "OK? Promise?"

I promise.

"Where's Stitch?" I croak sleepily.

He must be outside.

I can't see. I bury my head further into Mum. I don't *want* to see. There is smoke everywhere – big black charcoal circles of swirling hoops. It's so dark, with new horrible shadows leaping all around. I can hear the roaring flames whispering in my ears. I'm scared. I'm *so so* scared.

It feels hot and close as we move out of the flat.

It's a fire.

Our home.

Our palace is on fire.

I don't want to look.

We run out into the stairwell ...

I hear the blaring shrills of Primrose
Mansions' fire alarm. Our neighbours are also
flowing into the stairwell in their pyjamas.

They're panicking, screaming, shouting and running about, desperately trying to escape. Sprinklers hiss around us.

Where's Stitch?

"Where's Stitch?" I scream. "MUM, WHERE'S STITCH?"

A man is shouting, "DON'T USE THE LIFT!"

And Mum begins to run down the cold hard concrete steps with her bare feet slapping the ground. She won't let me go. She won't put me down.

She is holding on to me so tight and I am so scared and I keep screaming, "What about Stitch? WHERE IS HE? MUM? WHERE'S STITCH?"

And she keeps telling me not to worry. She keeps saying that everything will be OK. She keeps saying that she loves me very much. She

says she loves me very much. She says she
loves me.

But ... Stitch.

Don't you love Stitch? Mum?

What about Stitch?

Chapter 15

We clamber down, down, down, down the stairs. I am gripping the banister, desperately trying to make Mum go back.

She is shouting, "LET GO!"

"PLEASE, PLEASE, MUM, PLEASE …"

People are tripping up and falling around me. It's all so hot and fast. I feel sick. I am screaming for my baby brother's life but nobody is listening. Everybody is too busy listening to their own screams.

WHY IS NOBODY LISTENING?

And then suddenly we are out of the building and away from its licking flames.

Mum falls to her knees on the fresh green grass, panting with relief ...

And people wrap me in a blanket and take me away to check for injuries.

I don't want to be taken.

I just want Stitch.

Mum runs to me and is holding me and gripping my face and kissing me and crying.

"Please ... please, Mum," I say. "Tell them to go back inside and get Stitch. Mum, if you don't ... he'll burn."

"Sequin, it's time to let him go."

"Mum, I can't, Mum! You can't leave him, you can't, Mum. Please."

Two firefighters run over. "Somebody said they heard your daughter screaming for her baby brother," one of them says. "Is there a baby still in the flat?"

I look to Mum as tears roll down my cheeks.

Chapter 16

And then out he comes.

Moany Bony Mr Tony, coughing and spluttering his way towards us.

I BET IT WAS HIS FAULT THAT THE WHOLE BLOCK WENT ON FIRE! HIM AND HIS SMOKING! HE LIED TO US THAT HE WOULDN'T SMOKE, BUT HE DID. I KNOW IT.

"Sequin ... you're OK!" Moany Bony Mr Tony gasps, and he puts a bony arm around me.

And from inside his stinky rotten coat he brings out a floppy, well-loved worn rag doll. It's

made of odd ends and scraps. Rags and fabrics.
Wool hair. Button eyes and a strip of velvet for
a smile.

It's Stitch.

I want to hug him but I can't bring myself to.

He doesn't look the same to me any more.

The firefighters look confused.

And it all becomes real.

Chapter 17

Mum hugs Tony hard.

"That is the kindest thing anybody has ever done for us ..." she says.

Mum pauses, and then she speaks again. "When I was pregnant with Sequin, I was actually pregnant with twins – a boy and a girl." She looks at me and smiles but tears fall and her voice breaks. "The boy was born first, four minutes before Sequin. But he didn't make it ... he died."

I can't stand looking at Mum when she's sad, so I look at Tony instead.

"Sequin always wanted a sibling," Mum went on. "And so when she was old enough to understand about her brother, I told her about him. I told her that she would always have a sibling ... and we made Stitch. It sounds so stupid." Mum shakes her head, sobbing. "I can't believe you risked your life, Tony ... Did you think Stitch was ... *real?*"

"No," Tony says, "but I knew that the love Sequin felt for Stitch *was*."

Chapter 18

The giant's remote control is not grey and still any more but wild and angry. Red and yellow and orange flames are eating Primrose Mansions alive. There is black smoke circling into the night sky. Firefighters in oversized waxy jackets and hard hats are trying to kill the fire with hosepipes, as if they are blasting a monster with laser guns.

The heat is too much. We are safe outside but the flames are roasting our skin.

Teasing our hair like feathers.

And the *smell*.

It hits the back of our throats.

It makes us cough and choke.

It's the smell of burning.

And when the fire is gone, there is smoke.

Ash.

Dust.

Memories.

I find myself clinging to Stitch tight.

"Everything we had was in that flat," Mum says, sounding numb. "Now the princess won't have a dress. I won't have a job. We don't have a home ... We have nothing."

I look at my mum.

She is here, forced outside her prison as our palace burns down.

Perhaps we are more alike than I even realised.

The stitches are cut.

If she can let go …

Then I have to do the same.

It's time to say goodbye.

I breathe Stitch's familiar smell in for the last time.

I love you, Stitch.

And then … I unravel him. I unpick him, seam after seam, stitch after stitch.

I pull him apart.

And in the centre of his chest with the stuffing and fluff is a single sewing needle, exactly where his heart would be.

"No, Mum," I tell her. "We have everything we need right here. I am stitched to you. And I always will be. You *made* me, remember? We only need each other ... and *this*."

And I place the needle in her hand.

Chapter 19

The fire was on the news.

It turned out it was caused by a dodgy broken fan on a fridge on the ninth floor. Nothing to do with Moany Bony Mr Tony, who hasn't smoked one single cigarette since the fire.

"I saw you in the paper, Sequin," Teegan says. She's skipping over with a fake plastic grin on her face. "I can't believe you got to meet the princess. Did you really get to go to the palace?"

"Yes," I reply.

"Is it true that the princess's wedding dress burned in the fire?"

"Yes."

"Is it true that your mum made the princess an ice-cream onesie to wear as she walked down the aisle instead?"

"Ha ha. Yes."

"Wow, that's so cool. Is it true the princess is going to employ your mum full time to make all of her clothes?"

"Yep."

"Did she make that dress for you that you had on in the paper? It was so cool!"

"Yep."

"Woah! Can your mum make *me* a dress?"

"She *could*," I say. "My mum can make anything she wants."

Teegan's face lights up.

"It's just that she only makes clothes for princesses, you see?" I add. "Sorry about that, Teegan."

"But … you're not a princess," Teegan says.

"Yes, I am. My *palace* might have burned down … but I didn't."

And Teegan's jaw drops and she watches me run towards my mum. She's standing on the other side of the road, the wind in her hair making it fly like ribbons.

Our books are tested
for children and young people by
children and young people.

Thanks to everyone who consulted on
a manuscript for their time and effort in
helping us to make our books better
for our readers.